THE ANGELICS WIFE

L. A. STAFFORD

The Angelic's Wife

Memoirs of a Lyran, Angelic/ Human Hybrid

L.A. Stafford

The Angelic's Wife: Memoirs of a Lyran, Angelic/Human Hybrid.

Published by T.C. Stafford.
First Edition, 2019
Copyright ©2019 by T.C. Stafford (L.A. STAFFORD)

www.lastaffordauthor.com

Print ISBN: 978-0-6484325-2-4
E book ISBN: 978-0-6484325-4-8

No part of this book may be reproduced, scanned or distributed in any printed or electronic form without permission. Please do not participate in or encourage piracy of copyrighted materials in violation of the authors' rights.

These are works of fiction. Names, characters, businesses, places, events, locales, and incidents are either the products of the author's imagination or used in a fictitious manner.
Any resemblance to actual persons, living or dead, or actual events is purely coincidental.

Cover Design by Sly Fox Cover Designs 2019.
Edited by Vixen Publishing Australia 2019.
Formatting by Affordable Formatting UK 2019.

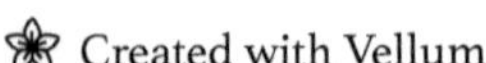 Created with Vellum

*FOR MY FRIEND RICHARD L HATCH,
WHO ALWAYS BELIEVED IN WHAT WAS BEYOND THE
VEIL AND WHO NOW LIVES WITHIN THE LIGHT.*

.

COMING SOON

The Ascension Series
Book 1
Cassiel.

The Angelic's Wife
Volume 2
The Reptilian Effect.

The following is a summary of various diary entries and thoughts over a period of eight years. They are personal experiences of my journey within the Matrix as I endure Spiritual Ascension. Any similarities of these experiences are purely coincidental.

THE ANGELIC'S WIFE:
MEMOIRS OF A LYRAN, ANGELIC/ HUMAN HYBRID.

Introduction

I knew there had to be more to this life than the routine I was living. I'd never quite felt what was deemed as normal. I had no idea what was out there just beyond what we spiritualists call, The Veil. I had no idea how my normal and practical little life would soon change.

Most of my life, I'd never fit in. I was always left out, belittled or told I was worthless. The journey I was about to embark on would show me just how valuable, not to mention, powerful I was; I'd just forgotten who I was. I guess we've all felt like that at some point. I'd just forgotten who I was by repressing hidden torments. I later learned why. My mother always told me I was worthless and may as well be dead for all the difference it would make! As I travelled many roads, enduring many experiences, death couldn't come quickly enough for me. I still pray for it on occasion.

My younger years were filled with violent and abusive memories as I lived in a household filled with fear. My mother, father and brother, a ginger cat named Tommo and a white Labrador named Pepper, all lived in suburban Brisbane during the 1970s.

My father was an extremely violent man who would beat my mother most days, be it with his fist or a wooden leg off the lounge chair. I can still hear her crying from the pain. Of course I loved her, and I spent my childhood protecting her, contrary to the lies and twisted stories that were eventually circulated to cover my family members' abominable behavior. I could never understand why she stayed as long as she did. Back then, it was known as "Battered Wife Syndrome". Nowadays, we call it "Domestic Violence". I later suffered the emotional effects of that in my 30s by allowing men to treat me in an abusive manner, or take advantage of me financially.

My mother's sadness was worn like her favorite red coat in winter. It literally became a part of her. The sound of my father's hands hitting her skin will stay in my memory forever and her memories of the past eventually drove her to madness. My brother would deal with it differently by running into his bedroom and turning up the music so he didn't have to hear the fighting. In his late teens, he began taking on the traits of my father, following suit with abusive behavior which would later be deemed as acceptable conduct. Who better than an abusive father to show his son how to treat women? His conduct hidden, it allowed his sociopathic personality to run wild, to deny his sister the ability to shine. She would be unloved, hunted down and hated due to twisted stories.

As the years went by and I entered my adult life, my childhood set a precedence for the type of man I would choose to be with in this lifetime. As my mother's mental illness surfaced from the domestic violence she endured, I became a reminder—a reminder of the past, *her* past. I was advised of the atrocities that brought me into this world and constantly reminded of such things as my adult life progressed. I suffered for what she endured. Mentally, I took the hit over and over. I learned many years later that there was a generational pattern for the women on her side of the family. They chose bad men who would one day perform acts of great shame, whether it be rape or violence towards women. She coped as best as she could, but it shaped how I viewed men for many years to come, as well as impact my self-worth.

As I travelled down the road of spiritual awakening, I learned that my bad experiences with relationships and friendships, whether they be violent or hurtful, were written to be experienced here—in this lifetime—because what I was living in another dimension, in another life if you will, was exactly the opposite. In that dimension, I was engulfed in pure bliss with the love of a being that would only re-enter my life when I was in my mid 40's. He connected with me in ways I couldn't have imagined. He was simply waiting for me to come home, and when I'm released from my contract and have fulfilled all of my lessons, I will go home.

I wasn't prepared for it, but I knew that unconditional and soul-knowing love was on its way in the form of a twin soul. This love would engulf my entire core—a knowing that I was one in union with another soul. I knew it in my Chakras, but I also knew it deep within my heart. It was within reach, just beyond the Veil. The trick was, how could I bring it into this third dimensional reality? How could I integrate with my higher self to experience such elation? How could I also stop living someone else's life? As I slowly peeled back the layers of "ME", it all became clear.

This is the journey of my Ascension into total bliss as I step into both 4D and elevate to 5D.

This is my journey home.

CHAPTER ONE

REBIRTH

So, what is it that we learn from the past? We learn from the experiences. We don't learn emotion. We don't learn heartache—we sure as hell feel it—but we do learn as a result from these experiences. This is all part of the Soul Contract within the Matrix. So, what is the Matrix you ask? My theory, and if you'd asked me last week, I would've said it's a very well camouflaged version of hell on earth! A hell that's designed to help your soul grow. Some also refer to it as a Prisoner Planet. It's a recycler where you're tricked and then recycled to enter into another life and another and another until your contract has expired. Well, this is my theory, but only on my bad days.

Try imagining an orange as God, or Creation as I refer to him. When Creation wants to learn, he breaks off a segment to experience in order for his soul to expand.

Then the soul breaks off another segment and so forth and so forth. Or imagine Creation as an infinite energy mass with millions of tentacles. Each of these tentacles has barnacles, and these barnacles are millions of threads experiencing life as we know it in any given dimension. They are all interweaving within each other. We are the barnacles. We are the learners. Interesting theory, isn't it?

I'd always believed in God, but not to the extent I do now.

Despite my turbulent childhood and the disturbing teenage upbringing due to my mother's hatred of me, I managed to get through it. I've always been told I'm strong. I'd have to be to have endured some of life's hardships, but I'm no stronger than any other soul here. I was yet to find out how strong I was going to become. I'd experienced major hurt from an early marriage and betrayal from friends who saw it as a right to take what was mine. My childhood abuse was well hidden by my brother, mother and her friends, creating in me a lack of self worth, a lack of happiness, a lack of value of myself and, of course, guilt for existing when others had passed.

In the years leading to 2011, I continued to push against those who tried to hold me back, knocking down the barriers until the universe decided it was time—time for my Ascension process to start. I was not by any means ready for what happened next. I'd been overseas several times, working in the sales industry with many colleagues sneakily stealing my commission and livelihood, making me work harder purely to gain back the money that had been taken. My body was physically exhausted. Looking back on it, it really was only a matter of time before it said *no more.*

Apart from the physicality's and the extremes of my working life, there was a great deal that was enjoyable as well. I was earning good money, but I realised I'd been neglecting other parts of my life. 2011 was shaping up to be one of my best years ever, or so I thought. I was on holiday with a Hollywood actor, who was filming on a cruise ship in the Caribbean. This man would eventually become a very dear friend. I was healthy, happy and in love with a man whose lies and the shock from them would later kick me into what the spiritual community call the "Dark Night of the Soul". In layman's terms, this is a process where your soul is forced to purge all that no longer serves it. It rids the darkness so that the light from Creation can anchor within. In my case, I cried for close to a year from all of my past hurts and the people and situations that no longer served me. Basically, I wanted to die! No, not exactly, but I did deal with much of what resurfaced from my life. And this can occur more than once. You will purge until the pain is gone and, of course, the lesson is learned.

That same year, I lost my beloved fur baby to the Rainbow Bridge after thirteen years together, my mother passed away and the man I loved let me down to the point where I could physically feel my heart break and my soul tear apart. I was also deceived by evil masquerading as a friend in order to get closer to Mr Hollywood! But the worst was yet to come. My family history of heart problems had finally caught up with me. I was on my way to work when my heart began to race and beat irregularly. After being admitted to hospital, I tested positive for coronary heart disease. I began to feel that I wasn't long from this world.

I was taken into the operating theatre in a wheelchair instead of on a gurney and as I travelled down the long corridor , I was overwhelmed with incredible fear. I knew I was going to die! I began to scream, holding on to the wall and beating it like a crazy woman, as if, for some reason, that would stop me from moving further down the corridor. The nurse did her job with a series of comforting words that calmed me in preparation for the cold steel slab I was about to lay on.

At least half an hour went by before the first stent was inserted into my artery. I felt the synthetic gadget moving in through to my heart. At that point, my body decided it didn't like it. The sensation of heat from the injected solution surged through me. The nurses rushed to get what I could see were paddles as the heart monitor let out a loud *buzz*. My arteries had shrunk, causing a blockage. The fluid they had used could not get through. I heard them say my name repeatedly. I then lost consciousness and flat lined. What followed next was remarkable.

I closed my eyes and woke in a vastness of black. I felt light as a feather. I was completely aware of who I was and the fact that I had died. I was surrounded by an endless black sea. There was no bottom and no top—just complete freedom. I felt my body being lifted through what I can only describe as a void of darkness. In the distance, and at the end of the blackness, were beams of crystal white light. They formed what most would describe as a tunnel. As I moved closer to the light, the crystal beams of beauty filled my heart with a complete knowing that I was in the presence of Creation. My ears heard nothing— just a deafening silence whilst I was being held in Creation's presence. As I was spoken to telepathically, and the rays of light glistened on my face, I was pulled back into reality. The feeling of complete peace and love was tremendous. I woke in my hospital bed, confused about what I had just experienced. I didn't understand at the time that I had just opened a doorway to another dimension. My second heart operation took place a week later.

When the doctors arrived, they explained what had happened; I'd undergone—and survived—a quadruple bypass. To this day, eight years on, I still feel like someone invaded my chest. I woke to gold light in my vision. I started to see odd things such as dark auras above the patients in the beds opposite me. I knew something wasn't quite right! My hospital stay became a distressing experience with many patients flatlining in front of me and due to my hysterical outbursts, I was removed from the room.

CHAPTER TWO

ASCENSION & THE DARK NIGHT OF
THE SOUL

On the way home from the hospital stay from hell, I was craving a McDonald's quarter pounder due to the level of salt I was lacking. I had literally had my insides cleaned out. After nine days of eating steamed hospital food, my arteries would have been smiling. So, I decided to dampen their spirits a little. I was desperate for a treat. What started out as a good idea ended with only a few mouthfuls being taken and the rest of the meal thrown out the window. I wasn't ready for that level of salt. It was a hard lesson to learn, of course.

Walking up the cement stairs to my flat was truly one of the most exhausting experiences I've ever had, not to mention, one of the longest. Going home after the bypass operation was definitely the best idea I had as the place was clean and the bed was made; however, my bed for the next three months would be the new leather lounge I'd purchased right before I lost my job for being sick. I was out of work for three months as I had to use the time to recover from the heart surgery on my own.

The little help I received was only a few days in total from those masquerading as friends and only until they couldn't get anything else out of me such as popularity and a claim to fame through association of my high-profile friends. I was too much effort. I was no longer fun or the drinking partner at the local pub. I was deemed as damaged. I became someone who they could control and whose life was destroyed through their jealousy of certain overseas associations. I would learn lessons out of this such as protecting certain public friendships and learning to navigate my way through social media, trying to avoid the green-eyed monsters around me. The mental anguish of losing loved ones equaled the physical pain I was enduring.

After being diagnosed with Type 1 Diabetes in 1978, I began to lose my blood sugar control. Complications from the heart surgery coupled with my family history of faulty hearts had caused several bleeds in the back of my eyes. The medical world calls this diabetic retinopathy. The doctors and I tried everything to gain better blood sugar control. I repeatedly had laser surgery to seal the bleeds, but the reality was, I was slowly losing my sight. Some days were better than others with partial or cloudy white vision, but mostly I couldn't see much. It reached a stage where three specialists finally agreed that I was going blind. It was just a matter of time.

That day, I left the hospital and headed home. I was sitting quietly in my lounge room, on my beautiful new white leather lounge that I would later have to sell to pay the rent, when I was engulfed by silence. There were no tears as there had been previously. In what I can only call a surreal moment, I began to talk to God. I stood up in the middle of my lounge room and stated, "I can't fight you anymore. Do what you want with me."

That was the moment everything changed! I had reached the absolute depths of despair, unable to see a future for myself. In fact, at that point, there was none. As I surrendered to God or whoever it was up there, I began to feel the room fill up like I was stuck in a crowd or a busy street. I could feel many a presence and I felt at peace. I also felt love. I knew straight away it was angelic. How? It was a simple knowing and I had felt it before. I had surrendered in order for God to guide me on a new path. Boy, oh boy, He sure did.

In the days that followed, and as I regained better control of my vision and blood sugar levels, I sat down and wrote at the computer with the magnifier on. Nothing Pulitzer Prize winning, but a story I would later be told was a past life and would connect me to the Archangels of Creation in ways I just couldn't make up if I tried. Most days, this would give me focus instead of tears which became an everyday occurrence. The depths of despair I felt is something no human being should have to endure. It left its mark on me and is something I will not forget in a hurry. I could also feel the presence of Archangel Gabriel, who I'd often call upon to help me write. I would later learn that it was quite the mix of several different Archangels who had actually been visiting.

So, with the loss of sight, the betrayal of friends, open heart surgery, financial loss, being hurt by someone I loved, several deaths and just plain bad luck, I ticked all the boxes that would kick me into Ascension. In relation to my spiritual awakening, I was definitely elevating at a rapid pace. At this point in time in humanities spiritual evolution many had started to elevate their vibrations to the fifth dimensional level. The pain and heartache endured during the process is referred to as the Dark Night of the Soul. A purging of everything negative, past and present.

I feel like my entire life had been leading to this. I had experienced betrayal in many ways. This appalling betrayal led me to alcohol and a feeling of self-loathing due to never being good enough. Death would have been a mercy considering the depth of my pain. Death was something I used to pray for on a daily basis. The impact on my worth was to the point where I let others dominate me or financially attack me as I unwittingly assumed that was how it was going to be. So, as expected, the Dark Night of the Soul revealed many past hurts, and brought out all the bad deeds inflicted on me. Of course, I had allowed these actions to take place, but they resulted in me being pushed to my breaking point. It was then that my life collapsed. However, in time, I slowly pieced things back together again.

CHAPTER THREE

MOTHER MARY, DREAMS AND THE VISITORS

As I slowly recovered from open heart surgery the physicality's and the daily slog became more difficult. I was forgotten unless I had the money to go out and socialise. Hiding behind my smile, I hid what made everyone feel uncomfortable—the truth. As time progressed, I encountered more animosity, hatred and jealousy from those masquerading as friends or colleagues. As mentioned previously, the Dark Night of the Soul brings forth all that no longer serves you. Learn to recognize it; you'll learn to forgive those who have done you wrong. You'll learn to let go of long held grudges and negative emotions. Negative friendships and situations are a good example.

My first experience with spirit was the appearance of Mother Mary. I woke to find a small woman around five foot tall, dressed from head to toe in white like a nun. Her skin, clothing and appearance were all crisp . She opened her arms to me, smiled and bowed her head. At that point, I honestly didn't know what to make of it. However, I did know I was being visited by a higher being. I felt safe and loved as she projected her energy towards me. In the days that followed, I felt lighter in both mind and body. I even walked with a spring in my step and Mother Mary in my thoughts as I endeavoured to progress in my 3D life as best I could.

Several days later, I was visited by my maternal grandfather. An elderly, grey-haired man, he wore a beige 70s business suit and held a brown paper gift bag. He presented the gift to me, leaving it on the end of my bed. I never did see the contents of the bag, however, metaphorically, I believe it held a spiritual gift of some sort. I never actually met my grandfather, but knew of the impact he'd made on my mother's life. She loved him dearly, but would find out decades later that he was not her biological father. Despite not being her blood, he was her father in every other way.

In June 2011, not six weeks before my heart surgery, I received a visit from my mother on what I now know as the night she passed away. Her vibrant, colorful presence, blue eyes and dark curly auburn hair that I remember as a child greeted me in my dream state. She was glowing, healthy and full of love. She took my hand and led me through white hallways. As we walked, I saw empty rooms, their walls stretching up to the sky. I felt safe, but I felt her purpose for showing me was to see that she was in her version of Heaven. There was no more pain, fear or illness for her to endure. She turned to face me as she spoke. I watched her mouth moving as I tried to understand the words but couldn't hear her voice. Then I woke up.

There is a Bible reference to Jesus and the white rooms of Heaven. I've not read the Bible, but I've been told by a friend that what I described was that dimension of love and light. Two days later, on the Wednesday, I found out my mother had died on Monday night—*that night*—the night she came to me. I felt a sense of relief knowing that she was now the being she used to be before the Matrix destroyed her mind—in this incarnation anyway.

In 2011, my dreams were so full of activity that I'd wake exhausted most mornings, or at anytime during the night. One that stood out amongst the others was a dream I later realised was not a dream, but quite possibly another experience from a parallel timeline.

The world was on the precipice of a world war. Great destruction was imminent. I had rescued an archangel. Taking shelter in a cave, I tended to his wounds. He had dark, shoulder-length hair and olive skin. He was partially dressed in a centurion uniform—red armor with a red sash draped over his right shoulder. His feet and hands had puncture marks from what looked like a crucifixion. The angel was not scared of me, but watched me closely as I placed a dish of water on the dirt floor to clean his injuries. As I wiped the blood from his hands, he said, "You are very kind."

I proceeded to the entrance of the cave where I watched the destruction of the planet. Many innocent and helpless souls had perished. The angel then took me in his arms, completely healed of all wounds.

His clothing and wings were all white and he declared, "My Father's hand will be swift."

I closed my eyes and when I opened them again, I found myself in what I can only guess was the entrance to the Crystal Palace of Heaven. The architecture was ancient yet beautiful, reminiscent of Roman gardens. I stood back and watched the angel speak with a female resembling a Greek or Roman goddess. For some reason she was familiar to me as well. I then heard her speak.

"You can't bring her here. She will have to go back."

I was then projected back to my bed, where I saw an elderly, white-haired woman look deeply into my eyes, and as she spoke, I felt an intense amount of fear at what she was about to do.

"We are giving this back to you."

She pushed a silver key into my chest as I screamed myself awake. The female I would see again. The angel would later show up in my life when I would least expect it.

I had always thought that life as a spirit guide must be a boring one with no communication between the watched over soul until they properly "woke up" and other angels. I remember when I first caught a glimpse of my spirit guide. That night I had stirred to the sound of feathers rustling. To my horror, I thought it was a bug in my room, but what I discovered had me giggling like a child. I found a beautiful angel whom I named Isabella, purely because she was too lovely not to have a name. Isabella had a small set of wings and was floating with her legs folded into a seated position as she read a book beside my bed. She looked to be in her 20s and had a lovely, peaceful aura of blue about her. As I watched her turn the pages of the book, I wondered what she was reading. I never did find out.

CHAPTER FOUR

VOICES IN THE DARK, THE WHITE BROTHERHOOD AND THE LYRAN ROYAL

After four and a half years in my apartment, I decided it was time to change the energy by releasing the negativity of illness and what no longer served me regarding people and aspects of my life.

I found a new apartment which would later provide a new path to my awakening process. After having gone through my first Dark Night of the Soul, my third eye was wide open. I was viewing my life differently. I was excited at the prospect of what I was embarking on—a spiritual life. I was beyond excited at the prospect of my blooming psychic awareness, but my cockiness and naivety would be my weakness. I learned that not every being in the universe is a friend of humanity.

Unfortunately, the dwelling I moved into was not what I expected. Poorly renovated, it hadn't been cleaned and the carpet was filthy. I was greatly disappointed in the real estate who proved to be less than professional in their approach. With my lease signed for twelve months, and after the heavy influence of a family member, I decided not to renew. However, what I experienced during the months in this rental were amazing.

My first night in the apartment was surrounded by skyscrapers of boxes. During the night, I woke to hear two women talking about how messy the place was, how many boxes there were and that I had my work cut out for me. Of course, I leaped out of bed, checking the apartment for what I thought were criminals who had broken in to steal something. After checking from top to bottom, I found nothing. No forced entry. No holes in the walls. No man holes in the wardrobes. Even the windows were too high up for anyone to break in. I went back to bed and as I lay there, I realised that the voices were quite familiar.

As my spiritual eyes took hold, I began to see flecks of silver light in my vision. I later learned these were my angels letting me know they were close by. I often said, "Angels, give me a sign." Without fail, I got the silver notifications within my sight. I started to feel the daily effects of the spiritual awakening as both my body and my diet were impacted. I began to eat less meat and more vegetables and fruit as that was basically all I could keep down. My body was physically rejecting meat and the vibration of eating a living thing was disgusting to me. Sunday morning bacon and eggs turned out to be a total waste of money and time as the moment I swallowed, it would come straight back up again.

One day, I decided to take myself to the movies and for an early lunch. I bought a roast pork sandwich with the lot —crackling, gravy and apple sauce. It looked delicious and I couldn't wait to demolish this masterpiece of greatness. I sat down to waste some time before the cinema session started and took a bite of the crackling first. I then received a message in my mind: *You're eating my skin.* I literally stopped chewing. I then took a bite of my roast pork sandwich, swallowed, then ran to the public toilets to vomit. I could feel the vibration of the animal and the fear it felt as it was killed. I began to eat off the vine—fruit and vegetables, nuts and small amounts of bread and cereals. No alcohol and lots of water.

The change in diet had certainly raised my vibration level, which permitted me to live in the fourth dimension. I had left the 3D world behind. A spiritual life had engulfed me, allowing me to enter into a world that was so much nicer than the one I'd previously been occupying.

I was now seeing cloaked beings. Around seven feet tall and dressed in both blue and red cloaks, they bowed to me once they had my attention. Spirit after spirit presented itself to me in human form before fading or walking away. I was woken two to three times a night in the early spiritual hours of sleep, while during the day, I received messages into my mind in the form of memories.

As the year progressed, I became aware of many

different types of beings in the universe. It reached a point where I was the main attraction of what was starting to look like a sideshow and I was the freak. It was not just exhausting, but my health was beginning to suffer from the constant waking up during the night. There was one particular being who visited that proved the most interesting- a Lyran. It's said that the constellation of Lyra is where all life began, where most species and humanity can be traced, included my own ancestry. This is a place where humanity's ancestry would originate and then form many hybrid races.

One night, I was awoken by a regal looking female being with long, luscious, dark red hair and yellow eyes. She had a slight cat face, but she stood tall and grand. I remember being extremely annoyed as it was going on the fourth time that night that I was woken from a very shallow sleep.

As she watched me, I yelled, "What do you want?"

I gave this being such a shock that her beautiful yellow eyes widened in surprise. She stood there, staring at me for what was only a few seconds then turned and disappeared. I felt she was of Lyran descent, but she seemed to be a full blood from what I had seen from pictures online. To this day, I wish she'd come back. To be in the presence of such a feminine being from another galaxy was energetically phenomenal.

Now, not all of this spiritual awakening was exciting, and I can honestly say that my true WTF moment shook me to the core. Imagine waking to what looked like six high priest/ pope-like ceremonial entities standing around your bed. They were all male, wearing white from head to toe and holding books in front of them as if they were reading some form of incantations. I was completely terrified. What on earth were these beings saying and what were they about to do to me? After some research, I found out they're known as the Great White Brotherhood. These are beings known as Ascended masters, who share their spiritual teachings and knowledge with selected humans. Soon after that, I saw a long golden haired being wearing a headdress and holding a wand. She looked like something from one of my tarot cards. The next morning, I woke to find a scratch on my forehead—a straight line like I had been marked for later use. I feared what was to come.

CHAPTER FIVE

THE GREY ALIEN, THE EMERALD TABLET, JESUS AND CHRISTINA

My knowledge of the grey alien beings was pretty much limited to what I'd seen in science fiction movies. ET the Extra Terrestrial was how I expected all greys to be—chatty, alert, highly intelligent and a little bit cute. Boy, was I wrong! Now, I'm not saying that these beings are evil, but a few years later into my spiritual awakening I discovered that they were emotionless worker bees (for a purpose that humanity was slowly having revealed to them). At the end of my bed, and to my shock, I saw a Grey. It was about four foot tall, and had large eyes. It stood there watching me. I woke the next morning with a blood nose. I was angry at the realisation that I'd had an implant inserted. It would be another twelve months before I experienced further visitations from them.

One of the more interesting occurrences was of the light language I began to see. Light language is a series of letters and symbols sent by beings from other galaxies, messages from ancestors and loved ones. It is communication. I started to see bright green writing on the walls of my room when I woke up. On occasion, I see red and green, but mainly black. I even started to see different beings writing on the walls, which became an interesting sight. My first vision of light language was florescent green and about the size of a scroll. It ran the full length of the wall and I later discovered it was the Emerald Tablet—teachings written by Thoth from ancient times. The light language varied and even on some occasions, would show coordinates from another galaxy.

On my bedroom wall, I had a framed spirit guide drawing of Jesus. I was always intrigued by how lifelike it was and how it was also a little like the Mona Lisa as His eyes followed me around the room. In fact, Jesus became one of my regular visitors. He would stand in the doorway and smile before leaving, which reassured me I was protected. To my shock, I started receiving visions of the Crucifixion. Not of the act itself, but of the surroundings and the mountain where it took place. I saw the path where Jesus walked to Golgotha whilst carrying not just the burden of humanity's sins, but also a very thick wooden stump that stretched across the breadth of his back from hand to hand. I saw the cobblestoned street that supported his footsteps and his face dripping in his own blood. His eyelids were swollen shut, his body beaten, bloody and bruised from head to toe. This vision was beyond distressing. I felt as if I was watching from the sidelines as he walked down the small street, the sounds of citizens screaming at him ringing in my ears. I remember feeling ashamed to be a human being. The crucifixion of Jesus has always shaken me to the core due to the barbaric nature of the act. Although through research of that time, I've realised that the fear of the people of Jerusalem during those early political times in our history fueled this brutal past in society's story.

On another occasion, I woke to find Jesus sitting beside my bed with several followers huddled in a group on the floor. When he got up to leave, I became upset and reached out my hand to him.

"Please don't leave me," I said.

He took my hand and smiled. "I'm always with you."

I was emotional at the realisation that this being is a part of us, as he is a part of Creation, and we are all children of Creation. To this day, I still see him hovering in the doorway, still catching my eye before disappearing into the light.

My mother was a different story. Her passing had been a relief, but it had also brought a lot of emotional baggage to the surface. After her visitation on the night she transitioned, I saw her standing at the end of my bed with her arthritic hands held in front of her. I saw the aged woman I had known towards the end. As I saw her in the robes of an angel, she floated to the ceiling. Her skin looked mottled and patchy, paper thin like a paperbark tree's trunk that had been picked at and carefully peeled away. It looked as if she was peeling away the remnants of her old body as she embraced her light body. The vision was stark and I was angry that she was elevating to a place of peace after the life she'd made me endure. I was a child of abuse and now I had to deal with the fallout. For a few years after this, I sought spiritual guidance from psychics and tarot readers. Of course, she came through in many of the readings, begging me to forgive her. I stubbornly said 'no' every time. I know at some point I have to deal with this, but I also know I have to go through the motions until I'm ready.

CHAPTER SIX

ARCHANGELS MICHAEL AND GABRIEL

I assumed that as word got out in the spiritual realm and the astral plane that I was able to see spirits and aliens, more beings would come as I built my connections with them. I began to see more and more angels. What was nice was that I was being watched over; I was being protected. I was becoming totally obsessed with Archangels and Angels. I honestly love these beings, but always wondered why I had such an obsession with them. This would be revealed to me later down the track.

Day in and day out, I saw spirits and beings from other worlds, like I was looking at a normal third dimensional being. As I laid in bed, not tired or close to drifting off, I relaxed and wondered what I would see when I woke during the night. Coming out of the darkness was a being resembling an x-ray of energy. It was cloaked, but not quite human. It was a male, but at that point in time, after seeing some of the things I had already seen, nothing frightened me... Not yet anyway. As the being came up close to my face, I asked it to be clearer. It then materialised into a swarm of color curling itself up into my neck. It stayed close to me. Overwhelmed with love in my heart, I couldn't do anything but cry as I was overcome with a feeling of complete love in the core of my being. This was the experience of a lifetime, but then it disappeared.

What happened the next night I won't forget in a hurry. I woke to find an exceptionally tall man stooping in the corner of the room I looked closer to find he was holding a huge sword, and he shone with a blue aura. I don't know if he stayed, but he was observing me quietly—watching over me as I slept. I knew straight away he was Archangel Michael.

The following night, I was just drifting off to sleep when, out of the darkness stepped one of the most good-looking men I think I've ever seen—well up until that point anyway. He had long golden hair past his shoulders, pale skin and the largest, most strikingly beautiful blue eyes. He was wearing a blue jumpsuit, with the shoulders of the suit covered in armor. He also had a long red cape attached to both his shoulders. He bent down beside my bed and looked deeply into my eyes. I could literally feel him looking into my soul. I was so unnerved that I screamed and startled the both of us. I don't know which one of us was more shocked. He stayed with me for a little while before stepping back into the darkness. I later found out it was Archangel Gabriel. He was larger than life and beautiful—so very beautiful.

I'd learned also that Gabriel was responsible for awakening my creative side. As a writer, you tend to pray for a muse to assist in all aspects of writing and communication. I guess an Archangel as a muse was pretty damn good. Funnily enough, I had a figurine of Archangel Gabriel on my work desk. I guess it worked.

CHAPTER SEVEN

A NEW ADDRESS, FURTHER AWAKENING AND THE LESSON

After a lifetime of manipulation and disrespect, I began to take back control of my life and of my spiritual awakening. The hardest lesson I'd learned was that when you allow others to sway you off your path, you live a life that is not your own.

I joined several groups on social media and began to learn a great deal about what was really out there. It was refreshing to match up what I was seeing with descriptions of intergalactic beings and other entities. I also moved to another apartment—a thirty-story block with an overwhelming energy. As I spoke to more and more residents, I learned that there were several ghost and sprit sightings. These were linked to a very dark past. I was advised that the building not only had a death on site during its construction, but the area itself, many hundred years before, had been an Aboriginal initiation ground where boys would become men as they hunted various animals, or began what our native Australians refer to as the rite of passage.

Several months later, I realised I shared an apartment with several spirits and entities. We came to a mutual understanding that I paid the rent—not them—so if they wanted to stay, they needed to keep their distance. However, I was struggling to set up spiritual boundaries and, honestly, I didn't know how. At this point they kept their distance from me, only observing me from the shadows. I was so brave. I was in control...or so I thought!

I started to get closer friendship-wise to a fellow group member on social media who would later show me the dark side to spirituality—how to set the intention of swaying someone's mind to have the darkest of thoughts to push me over the edge. The one thing Spiritual Sight teaches you is to be careful and really use your own discernment when it comes to teachings and guidance from others—to trust that inner knowing from inside. Where there is light, there is also darkness. I reached a point where my vibration was elevating rapidly, and I was fluctuating within 4D and 5D. Day by day, I felt my spiritual connection to the other realms expanding. There were days where I couldn't even walk straight as I endeavoured to get to my destination. My human eyes allowed me to see a distorted view of the world around me as it vibrated and shook between the two dimensions. When the lights went out at night, I saw a room full of spirit and entities swirling around. I would see portals like a special effects within a movie, only the movie was right in front of me and very real.

To my shock, in February 2017, I received the devastating news that my dear friend, whom I will name Mr Hollywood, had transitioned. As did most of us that knew him, I unfortunately found out via social media. I screamed uncontrollably. I felt angry that we had not sorted out our differences caused by jealous women who deemed his friendship as entertainment instead of seeing the soul and the great friendship that I knew. As my grief took hold, and my emotions tore me apart deep inside, I felt someone rubbing my arm to ease the pain. That night, I woke to a visitation from Mr Hollywood. He came to see me one last time. He was wearing his dark blue jeans that made him look like he didn't have a bottom, his classic red t-shirt and his black dinner jacket. I liked to see him in this outfit and he was comfortable just being a guy in a simple jacket and jeans rather than a dinner suit and performing the antics of the Hollywood actor. Maybe that's why he presented to me like that. I'd been speaking to him in my dream state within the astral before I woke, but I couldn't remember a single word he said. When I was awake, he smiled and turned to walk into the light. I'd now seen both my mother and Mr Hollywood walk into the same light and white surroundings like he was floating on air.

This also opened a door between myself and a mutual friend of Mr Hollywood's that I hadn't spoken to in several years. Let's call him Mr Unrequited! Mr Pain and Heartache and Mr Dark Night of the Soul, but mostly Mr Liar. I think most of us have met someone like this before. I'd unwittingly placed my heart in a holding pattern for ten years as I loved and forgave, and loved and forgave this desperately disturbed man. Our bond was our friendship and love for Mr Hollywood as we were also part of a specific social group that would holiday with Mr Hollywood. My journey within the spiritual world had led me to understand that I needed to cut the cords with him. I also had to ask myself what the lesson was. As the lesson became clearer, I learned to value my self-worth, keep my dignity and close the door to the past once and for all. Mr Hollywood's death finally gave me indirect closure—just not in the way I'd imagined. I hadn't realised it at the time, but this relationship had completely destroyed my heart. It hadn't been intentional, but I'd shut down and closed the door on love and relationships. This man, of whom I loved so deeply, I would now pray. I prayed for him. I prayed he could heal from his past and maybe one day learn from the lessons he'd been sent into the Matrix to learn.

CHAPTER EIGHT

ARCHANGEL CASSIEL AND THE ANGELIC'S WIFE

The first time I saw him, in this life, was during a group meditation at a spiritual convention, where we were taken on a journey with our higher self. I didn't really meditate much and didn't really believe that I was actually performing the task correctly. Plus, I had a bad habit of falling asleep during the process.

I thought anything was worth a try. I closed my eyes and let my higher self drift. I was instantly transported to a planet with two moons. It was night and the stars reflected off the navy-blue water. I walked barefoot along the shore to where a bare-chested, dark-haired male angel stood with his white wings unfolded as a lovely looking female with long dark red hair, pale complexion and a short white dress walked into his arms. I remember how wonderful it had felt and how when I opened my eyes, I thought I'd somehow been transported to another galaxy. I now know that this was a memory.

My next encounter came after an afternoon nap. I startled awake and as I sat up, I saw a seven-foot tall Roman Centurion with a red sash draped over his shoulder and chocolate brown hair that fell into ringlets on his face. The very presence of him almost made me scream. I felt his energy from across the room right before he faded. My first thoughts were, "Now that's cool." Of course, not knowing who he was, I guessed he had to be a ghost from the past.

That night as I lay in bed, a tall, long-haired being wearing robes appeared. This being had been watching me from the sidelines. I remembered that I had seen him a few years before when he appeared as both a swarm of color and also as a figure of a man visually as an x ray. I knew he wasn't a deceased spirit, nor was he what we class as an alien. He was a higher being.

I was full of questions and curiosity as I invited this being to sit next to me on the side of the bed. We chatted for what would have been thirty minutes. It wasn't a normal conversation; the energy being just nodded 'yes' and 'no'. As time progressed, I started to see my Roman Centurion on a regular basis. He was getting closer and closer to me. I guess he was lowering his frequency so I wouldn't scream as I had been known to do; it was a learning curve for both of us. I recall the night I woke to find him in full centurion uniform from head to toe, but what was different this time was that he was wearing his helmet (galea) with a red plume on the top. On bended knee, his golden armor shone like a diamond.

My psychic awareness was growing rapidly, but my connection to this being was still to be revealed.

Completely out of the blue, he surfaced during a psychic reading through a friend. What followed I didn't expect, but I was relieved to finally know who he was. He was the Archangel Cassiel whose role was to keep the flow of the universe moving, to observe and guide where needed, and to stand guard over Creation. This explained the centurion clothing he wore as he was God's protector. I was also able to remote view into other galaxies, viewing Cassiel standing before Creation. A small set of stairs lead to a huge energy mass—Creation and also known as God. He also revealed the name of my higher self to me. Funnily enough, I'd always loved the name that had been bestowed on me and I always wanted red hair.

It became obvious to me that I had seen my higher self as Cassiel fed memories to me. I was told that my tears attracted him to me, and the story I was writing had attracted the Archangels to my home. My writing had received cosmic attention—just not a Pulitzer.

As I mentioned before, I'd always found Angels and Archangels quite intriguing. My connection to these beings was strong. Although they knew I'd incarnated here, I guessed I looked slightly different to the woman they all knew. Time revealed me to each of them, but

Cassiel recognised my soul straight away. He stated that I had come here to be a bridge between humanity and the universe, and that many beings were aware of who I was.

The way the Bible wrote about these celestial beings was completely wrong in relation to how and what they really were. They could love and have children. They could have lives and fall in love—maybe not in the way that humanity does in this dimension, but there were definitely similarities.

As time went on, I was informed of many things. It was revealed that I was Cassiel's wife and the mother of his children. The names of our children were, funnily enough, my favorite names. Coincidence? I don't think so. This began to start my yearning to go home, the desire to be with my husband and my children, to be with my twin soul. Not being able to touch him in this dimension, or to hug my children, was and is still torture. Knowing they're always there within reach, but never to feel that touch, became more than I could bare.

I began to wonder what I was like as a being of light. What was I not achieving in that dimension that would warrant a trip into the Matrix. I started to question it over and over. The answer of course was soul expansion. To enter the Matrix during humanity's most important period of growth would once again prove how strong I was. How strong all souls that entered here were. I needed to understand that in another dimension, life was quite different. Although I was a highly-evolved and intelligent being, I was at a point where my soul had expanded as far as it could in the environment it was in. Can you imagine sharing a soul with a being who loves you, who knows what you need, when you need it and gives it to you? You then enter the Matrix to live an existence where your life has no happiness or love, no children, is filled with illness, betrayal, heartbreak and misery—the total opposite to what you had in the other life. How can you not appreciate or learn from that? That is the lesson in itself!

As my anger about being separated from Cassiel grew, it also began to grow to a different level of love. The feeling is difficult to describe but it was unconditional with a dash of knowing. As I would slowly remember our love and the feeling of his skin on my skin, it ignited a passion that made me long for his touch. I often found myself thinking of him and smiling. He constantly sent me visions of our wedding, of him wearing gold wedding clothes with myself dressed in the most stunning silver-blue Cinderella dress and my red hair looking like a meringue, all of which I found amusing. As my experiences grew with him, the intensity magnified. When I asked him to show me his favorite memory of us, I received a vision of my higher self with long dark red hair, standing in a field, surrounded by yellow flowers and greenest of grass stalks. I walked through the field as I basked in the sun as Cassiel watched my body sway with the wind that weaved through the field of flowers. As he showed me this memory, I cried. I still get emotional when I see it in my memory as his vision of me is completely engulfed in love—a love like I've never ever known.

Sometimes when I was cooking dinner, I saw him float into the kitchen. He'd watch me cook and I would unveil a culinary masterpiece (in my head it was, anyway). I received melodies and songs in my head. I knew he was singing to me. Some of the melodies were so angelic in sound that I doubt they could ever be duplicated here on earth with the exception of maybe Lisa Gerrard. Even now, I try to hum the melody. I long to hear his voice. I could always tell it was Cassiel by the distinct signs he gave me. He visited daily, materialising anywhere he wanted. On some occasions, he stood in the shadows at night, but when I called to him, he would pop out into my presence within a heartbeat.

Being a higher being, he didn't need a portal to visit me. Interestingly though, I had a portal in the bathroom which I found fascinating as I could see into another dimension. It quite often looked like a parallel world. If I got up during the night to attend the bathroom, I would always see a huge amount of energy activity as I looked around the room—energy beings moving in and out of the dimensional space.

Some of my visits with Cassiel were hours long and some just a quick visit. One of these longer visits was when I was lying on the lounge while Cassiel, dressed in his armor, floated above me. I saw him as clear as day. He was looking into my eyes as I was looking into his. I touched his cheek and watched his reaction to my touch as I cradled his cheek. I saw in his eyes the love he had for me. The vision of him was so extremely clear that I could see the lines in his irises. This energy exchange went on for at least an hour.

Several days later, my channeling friend delivered some quite specific instructions. He told me to only consume high vibrational foods such as fruit and vegetables, but to eliminate sugar, alcohol and breakfast cereals laced with sugar. This would help me elevate to Cassiel's vibration. I was told Cassiel would spend the day talking to my heart in order to prepare it for the love it was about to receive. I was also told to lay naked in my bed. He appeared, laying beside me. His purpose was for me to feel a vibrational connection to him through the energy exchange so I could recognise his touch when he was near.

The best way to describe this is to say it was as close to a tantric sexual encounter I'd ever imagine possible. I felt his energy move from my toes to my chest before centralising in my heart. Apart from the sexual energy, I also felt an immense amount of love from him. Vibrationally, the bond we shared connected us. I could send him messages and he, in turn, would send them to me. As time went on, he had his own pillow in my bed, but in this dimension, in the Matrix and in this dream, I was still alone and I hated it.

As the months went on, I began to gain weight. I honestly just put it down to my age and my heart medication. What was interesting though was I couldn't recall having had a period in many months. Back in my real life, Cassiel and I had two children—a boy and a girl whose names I am fully aware of. I've been told these two are very close. I guess with their mother away, they needed to be.

I was stunned, however, when one day Cassiel presented a baby boy wrapped in a blue blanket to me. I was later informed of his name. Our child was born within the astral plane and that, apparently, made him special. In a moment when I should've shown some form of excitement, all I could feel was anger. In fact, I was furious. I felt robbed and cheated of the opportunity to be a mother. My heart condition had unfortunately terminated my opportunities of motherhood in this dimension due to the bucket load of medication I was on to maintain a healthy heart. Obviously, our child was conceived with love and with my higher self in the astral. At this point, I was still viewing my higher self as the other woman.

I would have another astral child with Cassiel—a little girl conceived in a way that created a stronger bond. As I woke, and to my surprise, I saw Cassiel pushing the most elaborate and beautifully designed white pram toward me. He floated across the room and rested the baby beside me, and as I slept, he read a book. He was gone when I woke in the morning. Later, I realised he was trying to include me in all aspects of our family while I was away. Bless this beautiful being's heart. I was still in this life trying to get my head around the fact that I had an existence where I was loved beyond measure. I knew he would die for me and honestly, I would for him as well.

The light language on the walls was coming thick and fast and on occasion I would see Cassiel and our son writing messages on my walls. My desire to learn Enochian (language of the Angels) was on the rise. I worked out that if I told Cassiel to translate it into earth English that it would be easier for me to read. Ask and you receive...and I did. As more memories were fed to me, it helped create a stronger bond between Cassiel and myself.

As I longed to be with my husband and out of the Matrix, I became quite disconnected, falling into a heavy depression again. Originally, my experience within the Dark Night of the Soul had depression visiting me every day like an unwanted house guest. My channeler friend and I were discussing all things spiritual one day when Cassiel popped in. He wanted me to tune into him to see what he had within his hands. He'd brought me two gifts, both quite rare for an Archangel to give. In my vision, I saw Cassiel holding two white spheres. One had God energy (energy from Creation) and the other was his personal energy. He gave me these gifts so I could feel closer to him when I needed to feel the connection between us. The sphere full of God energy could be used by myself for a number of things. I could mentally expand the sphere to a huge ball of light and the uses would be endless. I could use the energy for protection, zap beings who would choose to harm me whilst in a state of vulnerability, or I could use it to expand the light around me for spiritual protection. Cassiel's energy would be different. On expansion of his energy sphere, I mentally found myself encased in a cocoon of safe keeping. That is where I would energetically go to feel his presence, to be safe or to simply feel his love. I still use it today!

CHAPTER NINE

ALIEN ABDUCTION AND THE REPTILIANS

During the months that my psychic awareness built, I started to see many different beings. My third eye was completely wide open. The moment the lights went off and I jumped into bed, the energy levels in my room elevated dramatically. One particular night, I'd just gotten into bed when I watched the walls of my bedroom morph into dark blue, metallic walls before my eyes. Thinking it was a kind gesture on my human part, I realized I may have possibly given the aliens permission to take me for a ride on their spaceships, accelerate the theft of my ovaries and abduct me into the alien breeding program. I thought this had been deemed as a learning experience for my higher self, or so I thought at the time. This is something I still struggle with and a concept I find disgusting to no end.

I realised I'd somehow been transported to a

spaceship. Looking ahead, I saw a T intersection, and in the middle of the intersection was an Arcturian being standing on, an electronic podium. Emotionally, I felt distressed. That distress only lasted a few moments though, because the next thing I knew I was back in my bed, the walls of the ship disappeared. A cheap version of Gandalf the Grey using a huge gong-type medallion with ancient markings on it sealed the portal shut. I shielded my eyes as there was a flash of bright light. When I opened them once more, there was a concerned look on the being's face. Floating closer to my bed, he checked to see if I was alright. I had absolutely no idea what just happened, but I knew I didn't like it one little bit.

This didn't seem to stop the aliens. I began to have many visits, which I found strange considering the efforts to seal the portal. On several occasions, I woke up in medical wards on ships, seeing scientifically advanced medical technology. I felt like I was having an out of body experience. I remember observing myself in the distance throwing up in a hospital bed. I saw different breeds of beings acting as medical staff. I witnessed other human females in distress in the beds beside me. I also saw a grey alien lying in a hospital bed only a few metres away from me. I was presented with babies of which I instantly rejected as the staff smiled at me like I'd just won the universal lottery. I was angry and I felt disgusted by these beings. I quickly realised what they'd done—what they'd been planning to do all this time: they'd taken my ovaries.

How dare they not ask me if I wanted to help their race by cross-breeding and splicing my DNA with another race. I didn't give my consent, nor did I at any stage feel this was acceptable. I did, however, feel like I had been organ ravaged and raped!

I knew my DNA had been taken. I knew my ovaries had been removed, aches and pains in my lower abdomen were evidence of that. I hadn't had a period in nearly six months. I found the only thing that eased the abductions was threatening to kill myself or yelling abuse at my higher self. I begged her to change the soul contract experiences that were written before entering the earthly plane for this lifetime. How could she do this to me? It must've been her… Right?

The ship events stopped, but the visits didn't—the species just changed. I couldn't understand how I'd become part of the Alien Breeding Program. I just knew it was wrong.

Cassiel's last visit was a few months before the Reptilians—a species that looked like huge lizards that stood upright—showed up. Some even had wings. They were called Draco Reptilians and were higher up the power ladder. When Cassiel and Archangel Michael finally came to me there was a feeling of concern at the time, but only now as I write this do I understand why. I knew something strange was going on, but I didn't realise it would be months before it would all be revealed to me. It was odd that both of them came to me together. I asked

Cassiel if he was alright. He nodded, mouthing the word 'yes', but there was no smile.

I had many nightmares of snakes and I saw reptilian beings every time I closed my eyes. As a green snake aimed to strike at me in my dreams, I jolted awake and threw my neck out. Two visits to the chiropractor later and I was on the road to recovery physically, but certainly not mentally. I saw groups of them standing around my bed, being signaling to go ahead to do whatever they did to me. I gathered it was feeding off my aura like the parasites they are. Unfortunately, they were also the reason Cassiel was away so much. They were stopping him from getting anywhere near me, blocking my connection to him. I was helpless—just human—and there wasn't going to be a rescue.

I was so distressed I shut down, closing the spiritual door. Despite my withdrawal, I still received visits from what I now know was a Naga being—an ancient being of reptilian descent who teaches those who are spiritually elevated in consciousness. Imagine a being with the head of a large lizard, arms and legs and wearing clothes like a space man. This one, however, kept presenting a child to me. I found these beings and the babies physically repulsive. I've read that many of these creatures are flesh eaters. I woke up many mornings and nights to find myself in a bed full of reptilian children. I was utterly disgusted.

For many months, I struggled, seeking advice from whoever would share information on the Reptilians with me. The visits and experiences escalated until a huge Draco being showed me a contract and pointed to the signature. It was trying to communicate that I was to provide them with my eggs against my will through trickery or worse. I also saw a sign on my wall saying "sex". Reptilians are known for sexual encounters with earthlings. Some attacks are reported to be violent and sadistic while others are said to be highly pleasurable. I woke up at night to witness them removing baby after baby from the lower section of my body. As they presented the babies to me, the human side of me couldn't comprehend how this was possible. I spat at these beings in disgust. I was supposed to acknowledge them. I was supposed to be happy about the mating ritual and the fact that these children were now in existence. In the early hours of the next morning, I viewed the same Draco being sitting in a chair beside my bed. He was standing guard over me, and every time I fought back, he presented me with the contract. The signature was unrecognisable; it was not mine. They had also taken to trickery by morphing into my angel statues to conceal themselves. After I worked out what they were up to, I started to mock them.

I managed to work out that their access to me was coming from a different level. I was still under the impression that my higher self was responsible for this. I later realised it wasn't my higher self doing this at all. She was receiving enough objection from what I was feeling to understand I didn't want this experience. I was in great distress and I began to see visions of my higher self-screaming. I needed them to understand that I didn't want this.

I eventually worked out that I needed to change my mindset; I needed to stop the effects of the reptilians. From then, whenever they appeared, I didn't acknowledge the babies. I rejected any contract made from trickery in the astral and dream states. I told them they were wasting their time, and more importantly, that they had no power over me. As they feed off anger, resentment and fear, I started singing every time I saw them. I chose a happy, jolly song that filled the room with love and joy. I even started saying stupid things such as 'I'm going to dress you in a pink tutu and you will look lovely.' Their constant smiling changed to frowns. Whenever I saw them after this, or when I was woken at night, I told them to leave—that they were wasting their time—before rolling over and going back to sleep.

For a short while it was working, but things were actually getting worse. I woke up screaming as alien baby after alien baby was taken from my body. I couldn't understand what was happening; I only knew I was terrified. I had to find out why I was being targeted. I pinpointed a time when I met a woman at a spiritual convention. I realized she'd targeted me once she found out my age and that I didn't have children in this realm. I needed help and I needed it fast. I finally found someone spiritually connected who knew what they were doing.

I sent Cassiel messages with the hope he could hear me away from the portals. As I walked into the store, the first thing she said was "Your angel is here and he won't stop talking really fast. I need him to slow down." I was so relieved I started crying. I told her I needed to connect with him for answers and that was when the truth came out. It was revealed that several contracts had been written and signed by this person for me to be part of the alien breeding program and that the ovary theft had taken place without my consent. This person had been psychically attacking me because she could see who I was. She had also torn my aura. There were three attacks from three different people. This, coupled with all the negative energy from both myself and the apartment block I was living in, worked like a lightbulb to the reptilians. They opened a portal for darker beings to access me in this dimension.

I was also advised that because these women were working with darkness, they had enticed the reptilian beings to hunt my children to the point where Cassiel had to hide them. His absence was now explained. Unfortunately, he couldn't juggle protecting us both.

These beings went after my children because I was a light being and they wanted me to raise their offspring which were made via theft and rape! It's almost like the theory of building a super advanced being like a super soldier. My Lyran heritage, along with my angelic/ hybrid

DNA had them drooling at the prospect of a race that would excel against others in the universe. Fear was setting in and when I could see them, they made sure I saw them licking their lips as they viewed me like I was dinner. How sci-fi it all was becoming, but to me it was simply disgusting.

When I arrived home, I wondered if they would try to attack again. As I woke during the night, I noticed Cassiel was with me. This time the Draco stepped forward again. It presented me with a video on small screen as they argued, They showed me a recording of a hand signing a contract. No picture of myself signing—just a hand—but presumably it was mine. I was once again shown a paper contract. This disgusting contract had a photograph of Cassiel and my new baby. I can only assume I was meant to offer my child as some form of sacrifice; Cassiel destroyed the contract in front of both myself and them.

I was told the only way to get rid of them was to make an offering. This offering would either be a flesh offering, like raw crocodile flesh, or a statue of a lizard or crocodile. I was given instructions to state the following: *All contracts and agreements made are now null and void. I terminate them. I would acknowledge them and thank them for wanting to give me this experience, but the answer is no.* I then told them to leave and not come back! Cassiel advised me to sage, cleanse and place symbols of protection on the walls for one month, and of course perform several protection rituals as well. The main thing I had to remember was to project love into everything I did and that would break the connections to these vile beings. I was shocked that they were bold enough to hunt my children. I woke one night to see them trying to take one of my sons again after it was born when Cassiel was visiting me. I viewed Cassiel taking off after them. I wasn't sure what happened that night, but it was revealed to me later. I was shocked and angry to be quite honest but I can assure you, hunt my children and I will call on Creation and my Lyran ancestors—not to mention the legion of Archangels.

The next night, Cassiel came to my rescue again when I screamed out for him. I'd told them *no* in very strong terms, but they presented Cassiel with yet another contract, this one with a photograph of our new born daughter. God only knew what it said. Cassiel dealt with the issue swiftly, bringing in another angel to help as I watched him give what looked like an order or form of instruction to another angel. I watched them bow in acceptance to Cassiel's instruction. I had a great night sleep the following night—the most peaceful I'd had in months.

I continue to sage and cleanse my home, but I'm very careful with who I allow into my friendship circle. It does leave me very guarded. I'd trusted and the result was unintentionally placing my children in danger. I've since removed myself from all social media groups to do with spirituality. I will no longer allow these attacks, or tolerate the terror of these beings.

Cassiel's message to me was that he was sorry he couldn't protect us both at the time and that it wasn't my fault for trusting these people within the spiritual community. Our children are now safe. My aura was repaired, a higher sound frequency was made and I was given instructions to follow as Cassiel healed me. Sometimes when you have no one to talk to about what you are going through, you will accept anyone that listens. My advice is to keep your eyes open. The lesson from this was to use my gut instinct and to listen. Life within the Matrix is difficult enough without also having to deal with spiritual Ascension.

CHAPTER TEN

ONLINE MESSENGERS IN THE THIRD DIMENSIONS

After my stressful Reptilian encounters, Cassiel began to show himself again. I received a kiss and it was welcomed although there was still no explanation as to why I had to experience such terror. How was this part of my Ascension process? Was this a test, or was it just bad judgement in trusting those in the community who would make it their mission to do evil amongst us? I do want to stress that not everyone in the spiritual community is like this. There are some wonderful teachers and lightworkers who work with us to help elevate the vibrational frequency of the planet. I just pray no one else has to go through what I did.

The Reptilians had created a barrier between Cassiel and myself, virtually blocking my connection to him. Due to the trickery of the Reptilians, I didn't know who was who anymore. To get around this, I asked Cassiel to come to me in a manner only I would recognize. A form that would be familiar to me. As the constant flow of visiting spirits was now a thing of the past, Cassiel would show himself and I knew he was with me every night. He would always give me a sign that he was near. When I woke in the morning, I would watch him disappear. His signal to me would become something familiar—something that helped me feel safe again. I could now sleep with the knowledge that I would be okay.

Sometimes I saw beings crossing out his messages on the walls. They were now seemingly trying to block messages from him as well. The Reptilians did everything they could to gain sole ownership of me, including placing a wedge between myself and Cassiel by showing me an image of him kissing another angel. Although distressing, it took me a while to figure out that wasn't the case at all. Their purpose was to gain power over me, my thoughts and my body. It's quite laughable to think they could possibly destroy the love between twin souls. This is where I gain my strength.

My channeling friend, who I'd met via social media, had gotten to a point where she had aligned with her higher self. She advised me that a being of her intelligence would never come to the Matrix, but did so to help me in my journey. Emotional blackmail message number one! She wanted to get rid of me. She also blamed me for this, for her being here and not there. This also meant she had left her Pleiadean husband and their children behind to enter the Matrix. Little did she know, he was reptilian also (a little something she can figure out for herself in due time). She also gave me my death date via a video she made me. This information caused me to have a meltdown as I crashed. This person's purpose was to manipulate, hurt and control—a game I wasn't going to play—so I walked away. No lightworker will openly give you a death date. True spiritual beings and psychics will tell you that you have quite a bit to do yet, or that it's just not your time to go. They will NEVER openly contact you, or record a video, to tell you that you will die in approximately eighteen to twenty-four months!

I had another friend request from an individual on another social media platform stating that Mother Mary had asked her to Friend me. She told me she was from Canada and had met Mr Hollywood. She told me I was part of the Alien Breeding Program and that she was powerful enough to stop it for me. I was so distressed with the situation that I accepted any help that was offered. However, I was way too trusting and naïve. She knew what she was after by accessing my social media profile and went straight for my photos. At this point in time, I was so distressed, I welcomed anyone who could help with the Reptilians. The stories came thick and fast, but the worst was the channeling of my dear friend Mr Hollywood, and the manipulation she was endeavouring to perform on me! Once again, I automatically assumed that if you were in the spiritual community, you could be trusted. I decided to close the door and walk away. It was too much. As stated in the previous chapter, I had no idea that her purpose was to tap into my own personal power/light in exchange for whatever it was that the Reptilians had agreed to give her. Sometimes they promise stronger or heightened psychic awareness, or just an acceleration in your abilities. She'd obviously signed the contract, not me; my aura was torn.

One after another. One manipulator after another. One spiritual attack after another taught me a lesson in judgement and trust. Many psychic readers after this experience brought Cassiel through and into the reading. They confirmed he was angelic, the love we shared was strong and that he was always with me. They said that although he was growing impatient for my return, he supported me and my journey in every way as it was what my soul needed. He knew life within the Matrix was not an easy journey. At least in that I have the faith to know the love I feel for him is real and the love of twin souls.

It also made it difficult for any other man to get my attention romantically—not that I wanted it anyway. The love of an Archangel is a hard act to follow. We human beings really have no idea what real love is. The love we experience here in this dimension is but only a fraction of the love we experience from Source/Creation. These psychic readers also went on to confirm the existence of our children, but they also confirmed the Alien children, the abductions and psychic attacks as well. My heart was broken, but I'm currently healing from all of this.

As it all came full circle, I began to realise why I'm here —in the third dimension and away from those I loved. My connection to Cassiel allowed me to view him remotely, standing before Creation and thinking of me as much as I was thinking of him. I never really experienced real love until I felt the connection of a twin soul. I experienced a bad marriage and bad relationships here in this third dimension, but I never really understood deep love until I felt it from this being. Many think they know and understand what love is, but the real knowledge of love is deep within the soul and at the core of creation. It's at the core of Creation that we find the desire to become more than what we are. This is why we become human. This is what Creation wishes for us, and this is where the fractal expands from the experience. Then, when the contracts are fulfilled, the fractal integrates back into the higher self.

Somehow the darkness I'd experienced from the Reptilians and the Greys had blocked my Ascension process. I could still see energy and was woken by beings from other worlds, but things were different now. I also lost trust in my angelic team; I felt completely abandoned. I knew I needed to build that relationship up again, but how do you do that? Well, you trust in them, you love them as much as they love you, and you ask for the help. After all that's what they are there for!

I felt like I was wasting my days. I longed to go home to my dimension. I also know I'm stuck here for a little while longer and not the eighteen to twenty-four months like I was previously told, but I know Cassiel will be by my side the entire way. I often wonder why I was woken up now and not when I was closer to transitioning. I realised that humanity as a collective is enduring individual Ascension, whereas before and many periods in time, humanity has ascended together such as within the period of Atlantis and the Mayans.

With the realisation that the Reptilians had tried to steal and harm my children, it shocked me into another shift of consciousness. I now feel Cassiel close by most of the time. He is here, protecting me. I understand a lot more and fathom that we are naïve beings to believe that we're the only race within the solar system. If humanity truly saw what was out there, I believe the planet would have a mass shift into fear. I now know that this is a dream —a very well programmed dream. The Matrix is designed purely for soul expansion. It's the longest sleep you can have. In a lot of ways, I feel like Sleeping Beauty waiting for her prince to save her. I also feel like I'm being held prisoner, enduring dream after dream, experience after experience.

My psychic sight has been temporarily placed behind a glass door that I will open only when I feel safe enough to use it again. I know it's there still, but I have to be careful now. After this experience, I'll think about who I was and what my lesson was for this lifetime. It seems there are many.

CHAPTER ELEVEN

THE MATRIX AND THE WISH

In more recent weeks, I've been able to connect with Cassiel on several occasions. He even brings our oldest boy to visit, who waves at me from within the Veil. I witnessed Cassiel in his Archangel form, complete with a huge set of beautiful white wings. He constantly stands guard at my bed and most nights I see him physically blocking the beings who try to bring their hybrid children to me. There have also been occasions where the Reptilians have allowed other beings to perform surgery on me.

I was woken one night to see the Draco Reptilian that had been attacking me, holding a poster of a picture of a heart. He was pointing to it. I then saw him holding a hybrid child in his arms and smiling at the poster, whilst another explained what was going to happen. I knew I was in trouble and was terribly scared. The next night, I woke to a Mantis being performing heart surgery on me. Mantis beings are exactly how their name sounds. They look like a really tall Praying Mantis insectoid. Having previously experienced the pain of open heart surgery, I recognized it immediately. I leapt out of bed and cried on the lounge until I fell asleep. I can't begin to tell you how scared I was.

When I woke, I was surrounded by all of my hybrid children along with the Archangel that Cassiel had given orders to previously. I guess he didn't get to me in time. I'm now once again concerned that I've been impregnated and will have to endure the pregnancies again. I've since asked Cassiel to advise Archangel Raphael to rid my body of these pregnancies. A few nights later, the Mantis presented itself to me again. I went through the spiel of telling it that all contracts were null and void and that they must respect my wishes and leave me alone. Although the Mantis being frowned, I haven't seen it since. There seem to be new Reptilians and a few other species appearing each night, however, Cassiel's protection symbols—which are now a permanent fixture on my walls—are a declaration to all beings who enter my home that I'm under Archangel protection.

Despite that, I've still had them try to trick me with the vision of Cassiel on his knees in front of what looked like the Reptilian King. A sword was put to Cassiel's throat. I was then presented with the body of my husband. My shock was not that Cassiel was dead, but that these beings were going to try everything to get me back to being their ovary mule! Of course, Cassiel is not dead as I'd know in my heart if he was. He's an angelic being and immortal. I've seen him many times in his true form. Although I feel the trickery will get worse, I also feel they won't give up—probably not until I can't have children anymore anyway.

What I know for sure is that the Matrix is a mass of different experiences, all individually designed to stretch the consciousness of a light being whilst being trapped in a human body. We only become a human when our light bodies inhabit the skin suit. We agree to sign a contract to enter the Matrix and we endure many experiences which are reviewed after each transition. There's no manual with this. No instructions. The Matrix exists and for those who are aware, you can actually see the grid and the symbols of the Matrix when you close your eyes. Or maybe that's just me. In order to grow, we're basically put into a deep sleep. We are given amnesia as we enter the earthly realm. It's like being placed into a maze and you have to find your way out. You literally have one foot in and one foot out—one foot in your real dimension of existence, and the other foot in the third dimensional world. You have two lives and two jobs. You are separated from the ones you love.

After the last year of my life here, I have seen the worst side to the universe as the Reptilians tried to overpower me. The realisation that they tried to take my children and harm them is beyond anything I can comprehend. It hurts my heart to know that Cassiel was forced to choose between me and our children all because of the antics of several women on social media. A lot of what I experienced was blocked from him as he couldn't break through the barriers they'd set up. This barrier will never ever be between us again. In fact, it has made our bond stronger.

When he was able to return to me after my aura was repaired, I saw him fight for me. He defended me and rid my home of the Draco Reptilians. Archangels love and desire and can have children, but if you go after their children or the woman they love, they will fight back. As for me, these beings need to be held accountable for what they've done.

There is a group of beings known as The Ashtar Command and the Galactic Council. I quite often now call on Commander Ashtar Sheeran for protection. The Reptilians and the beings who tried to harm me *will* be held accountable. The Archangels will not forget this and neither will I. The knowledge that not every being in the universe is loving and comes from a place of goodness is something we learn as we go through the Ascension process. I can honestly say it's still a huge shock to me. Even now, I don't quite feel safe as I write this passage, but I do know that Cassiel is by my side every step of the way. He is my protector and my love. He is my heart and my soul.

Celestial beings known as Angels and Archangels really do exist. The veil that separates us from our world here and the real world—the world we are *really* from—is very thin and if you are smart enough, you can penetrate that barrier. My alien encounters to date have left me with a sense of major trepidation. I'm hesitant to connect and use my remote viewing abilities and also my connection to spirit. I won't place my children in danger again. I will, however, learn to use these gifts in a different manner with Cassiel's and the help of the Archangels'. With a really great mentor, I'll grow as the knowledge will come from within the light and not the darkness.

When I think of the terror of when I saw myself screaming or when I saw my higher self being comforted by Cassiel after the experience of an attack by the Draco's, I'm left with the knowledge that within the Matrix is a tapestry of interwoven experiences designed to expand the consciousness. But there are also dark forces that enter the grid to destroy your souls expansion. To stop it. Most of these are Reptilian.

What I experienced, I wasn't meant to go through. It was not my higher self's fault—not in any way. I'm not exactly sure how I feel about things now. This experience has shaken me to the core. I know Cassiel is by my side and our love is perhaps stronger now than it has ever been. My Ascension has not been an easy journey. I've learned, however, that my soul contract for this life is to experience the many issues that we all struggle with as humans: love, trust, and honesty. I am also here to experience the love of an Angelic being whilst I am human. This relationship is certainly a challenge and the many books of knowledge I will write will also help others with their own Ascension process.

I currently feel as if my life before 2011 has now ceased. It's like experiencing a death of such, but my new life began when my heart stopped during surgery. This was when I began to "wake up". I feel like I have one leg in and one leg out as I experience life within this dream. I feel that I am in two dimensions, and the Matrix is where we learn our lessons. After being shaken to the core and woken up, I will now endure my time here. It feels like a prison, especially after what happened most recently. I'm fully aware of who I am from a heightened level of consciousness. I pray for an exit point so I can be with my husband and children. While I wait, I'll find a life that raises my vibration and helps me remember more and more of who I am. I now live in fear for the moment I transition. I will be tricked into coming back and enduring my long sleep over and over again. I know and understand that I need to work past this fear as it will keep the Reptilians close.

Many will question why I've chosen to openly and publicly share my experiences. I risk public humiliation and isolation, but my story needs to be shared within the spiritual community if only to protect the light. Others also need to heed the warning of how to acknowledge your true divine nature without the trickery. In this world, this third dimensional world, we judge anything that doesn't resonate with us. My purpose is not to stand here and make you believe me. My message is that you aren't alone and we all will, at some point, look beyond the veil and remember who we are. We will remember.

As I place together and remember the pieces of my real life, I have good days and bad. Ascension for me has not been what I expected. I'm still fighting against the system. I know in my heart that the Reptilians will not give up on the attacks. Being angelic myself and having Lyran descent, I'm like a free drug to a drug addict—a smorgasbord of light and energy. I am the fix they need. I now have visions of my higher self-asleep in a cryogenic tube—white jumpsuit and sound asleep. I'm guarded as I endure Gaia and the Matrix and dream of the day I can run through fields of flowers again whilst looking into the sun. In the distance, I will see Cassiel smile and I will be whole again; I will be home.

Cassiel awaits my return.

TO BE CONTINUED

ABOUT THE AUTHOR

L.A. STAFFORD commenced her own Ascension process in 2011. Although a bumpy ride, she has learned to take each day as it comes. Now residing in Brisbane, Australia, she is currently completing a legal degree. She spends her spare time writing paranormal romance novels focusing on Archangels and the love of Creation, often blending her many experiences within the spirit world into these novels. Her next work and the first book in her new series— The Ascension Series—"Cassiel", is due out in 2020.

For more information on L.A. STAFFORD please visit www.lastaffordauthor.com or for contact and event bookings tcstafford1@outlook.com .

You can also find her on: Facebook as @AuthorLAStafford Twitter as @LASTAFFORDau and Instagram as @authorlastafford

www.ingramcontent.com/pod-product-compliance
Lightning Source LLC
Chambersburg PA
CBHW071542100726
47908CB00004B/1478